THE GAME CALLED

UNIVERSE

THE GAME CALLED UNIVERSE

What If We Are Living Inside a Simulated Game and Our Thoughts Are Injected by Players?

Arthur Nawali

Allysol & Co. International

Published by Allysol & Co. International

First Edition

Contact: contact@allysol.com

Bong & Ally

TABLE OF CONTENTS

CHAPTER 1
The Influence We Don't See

"From the outside, it is a pattern; from the inside, it is chaos.
And yet, even chaos has its design.

Even in apparent disorder,
each story moves toward its own hidden harmony."

The Nature of Thoughts

You wake up one morning with a strange urge.

Nothing dramatic, nothing loud.

Just a quiet feeling telling you to take a different route to work, or to check your phone one more time, or to speak to someone you usually ignore—like your mother, for no apparent reason.

Sometimes you suddenly feel like taking a drive, breathing a different kind of air, or you don't want to get up when the alarm rings and bargain with yourself for just one more minute.

Sometimes you want to skip work without knowing why, and other times you wake up bursting with energy, ready to face everything.

And occasionally, for no reason at all, you decide to open a bottle of wine and let the day pass gently.

Most of the time, you don't question it.

You act.

And life moves on.

But what if that small urge or feeling was not random?

Patterns in Coincidence

About a decade ago, I read about a man who missed boarding an Ethiopian Airlines Flight. The plane took off normally, and then, within minutes, began spiralling out of control, plunging toward the ground before anyone could make sense of what was happening.

All 157 people on board were killed. But that man? He wasn't there.

Maybe he left home a little late. Maybe his cab got stuck in traffic. Maybe—just for a moment—he felt he should slow down that morning. No one knows. He simply didn't make it.

There was also a Pakistani expat in Dubai who suddenly felt like buying a lottery ticket at the Dubai Duty Free—something he'd never done before.

On a whim, he picked up a ticket, and it turned into a million-dollar win. Why did he feel the urge that day? Was it instinct, or a flicker of curiosity? A gentle nudge from somewhere he couldn't possibly explain?

It's intriguing. Or is it?

What do these feelings mean?

Are feelings and emotions just random ripples of the mind?

Or do they point toward something else—something subtle, something hidden, something guiding us in ways we never fully notice?

Is there a story behind these moments, one we haven't been told yet?

Henry and the Storm

Henry Foster was an enthusiastic car mechanic, living a calm, normal life with his family—a loving wife and two children. Wanting a short break from their daily routine, they decided to take a holiday to the Himalayan foothills, where they joined a campsite to spend the night.

During the night, a powerful storm hit the mountains, and Henry got lost in the mist of dust and snow.

When the storm settled and it was almost morning, Henry found himself alone. Terrified and confused, he walked along the hills calling out for his wife.

Suddenly, a few rough-looking village hunters emerged and overpowered him. They asked why he was there alone and shouting, but Henry couldn't understand their dialect. He tried to explain that he had lost his wife and children and that there were many people camping nearby, but he couldn't find them.

The men looked at each other in confusion, unable to understand a word he said. They captured him and took him to their small, hidden village near a lake in the mountains. Henry kept pleading with them to let him go, insisting that his family must be searching for him.

When they reached the village, Henry was taken into a small room where an old monk sat in deep meditation. Henry narrated his story, but the monk could not understand him, so he called for a young woman named Aloha.

Aloha was young and beautiful, with bright blue eyes filled with intense curiosity. She looked thin and serious, her ambition showing through calm eyes, a pale, worn scarf resting lightly over her head.

Through a rare cognitive anomaly tied to cross-world perception, she understood Henry and told the monk, in their dialect, that Henry was a *Crosser*—someone who had crossed from another world.

Aloha added that Henry was not from *Venna*, the world they were living in, and that he must have come from one of the other three worlds created by *Seranagu*.

Henry stood there completely clueless, trying to make sense of what was happening to him. But far beyond his understanding, something much larger had already been set in motion.

The Game Called Universe

When the game plan was revealed for the first time, word spread instantly like wildfire, and everyone was talking about it.

Some argued fiercely about the morality of it all—this and that—whether this should even be allowed. Yet beneath the noise, most people felt the same unsettling truth: this was inevitable.

The idea of building an everlasting, self-evolving, and self-sustaining platform called the *Universe*—capable of hosting infinite environments governed by only a handful of simple, fundamental rules—wasn't exactly new. It had hovered in theories and discussions for years. But turning that idea into reality? No one imagined it would happen so soon.

But then, it did.

The first stable build was launched with a pre-loaded environment named *Earth*. It was initially released as open-source, serving as a template for serious game developers to develop their own Universe-based games upon, before being quietly retracted due to ethical concerns over unauthorized simulations that violated core autonomy and existence protocols governing sentient character simulations.

Earth itself was a masterpiece of environmental simulation—self-evolving, self-balancing, and so wildly diverse that it could support almost any imaginable form of naturally simulated existence.

Oceans ranged from shallow coral gardens to unfathomable trenches; mountain chains gave way to endless rainforests; scorching deserts stretched alongside rolling grasslands wider than imagination; and frozen regions existed where time seemed to breathe in slow motion.

Everything was designed to serve one core purpose: to create a sustainable home for every type of character that could ever be developed, and to generate all types of qualia they required.

Qualia, as they called it, was the measure of emotional influence a player could transmit to a character during a game session.

Every game on this new platform now followed a sophisticated grid intelligence framework called the Cognitive Influence Simulation Protocol—designed not merely to control characters, but to shape their inner experiences through its inbuilt Emotion Engine and move them forward to execute a strategic game plan.

The stronger the emotional coherence between the player and the characters they influenced, the richer the qualia, and the easier the execution of the game plan—rewarding both the player and the character in their own terms.

Earth, with its boundless variety and elegantly interlocked systems, was the perfect stage for this new kind of gameplay.

* * *

CHAPTER 2

The Illusion of Randomness

"To walk in the dark with ease,
you must first lose your sight.

For only when certainty dissolves and the mind no longer clings to what it thinks it knows does your true vision awaken."

Limits of Perception

When a system becomes complex beyond comprehension, everything begins to look random from any local perspective.

This is not because the system lacks order, but because the observer lacks visibility into the countless interactions shaping each outcome.

In a world built from billions of choices, collisions, and subtle signals unfolding at once, even the most structured processes appear as noise when viewed up close.

Randomness becomes the name we give to patterns too large, too deep, or too interconnected for us to see. It is not a flaw—it is essential for challenge, growth, and meaning.

If every event were predictable, if every cause led to a guaranteed effect, existence would collapse into a script.

Without uncertainty, there would be no strategy to master, no adaptation to make, and no experience to learn from.

A world without randomness would be a world without depth.

The Simulation Protocol

To create the unpredictable at a scale of complexity no system could fully comprehend, the Universe Framework adopted a new simulation protocol called *Natural Simulation*, built upon the core principle of Autonomy of Existence—meaning there would be no interference once the simulation started, unless absolutely necessary.

The idea was to generate an entire simulated universe starting from an Initial Information State—a data set used to generate the entire simulation from zero.

From this state, simulated matter interacted naturally following just a handful of fundamental rules.

The entire purpose of developing the Natural Simulation protocol was to create something out of this uncertainty.

By dilating both space and time by millions of folds and allowing simulated matter to interact under only a minimal set of rules, the developers ensured that complexity would grow beyond any observer's comprehension.

From any local perspective, this complexity becomes indistinguishable from randomness.

It was the only way to produce a world that felt alive.

The Base Code

Beneath this apparent chaos, however, the Universe was never truly random, nor without rules. It was guided from the beginning by a predefined instruction set called the *Base Code*.

The randomness we observe therefore is an illusory experience born from limited perspective. What seems chaotic on the inside is coherent from the outside. This gap between global structure and local perception is what gives rise to probability - a method to access paths through randomness.

And within the characters that emerge out of this randomness, this concept of probability transcends into something called *Emotions*—internal signals shaped by uncertainty, designed for survival and decision-making.

Fear, desire, curiosity—these are not arbitrary feelings. They are evolved probability calculators or intuitive engines that help characters navigate an unpredictable world without ever seeing the full map.

From the player's perspective, this uncertainty breeds new challenges every day. Without uncertainty, there is no risk, and without risk, there is no triumph.

The thrill of navigating the unknown comes from the space between what we intend and what actually unfolds in the game.

From the very start, the Universe followed a guided framework, with galaxies, stars, and planets emerging through a broadly preconfigured Natural Simulation pathway—yet to any observer from inside the Universe, everything appears scattered and unpredictable.

This illusion arises because to any observer with partial knowledge, complex processes naturally appear probabilistic.

It is intriguing that even deterministic systems can appear random when viewed with incomplete information.

What we experience as randomness is often the shadow of deeper patterns that lie beyond our immediate perception.

The Challenge of Uncertainty

In a reality where outcomes emerge from a storm of probabilities, instincts, and independent wills, both players and characters are humbled by the limits of what they can truly know.

This uncertainty of actual outcome compels players to refine their intuition, to read subtle signals, and to accept that guidance is not ownership.

Just as it is for the characters within the game, players may choose, attempt, and hope—yet outcomes will always contain an element beyond their reach.

In that gap between intention and result lies the core challenge of the game.

If randomness were removed, the world would become static and predictable. Evolution would halt, creativity would vanish, and every character's fate would follow a predetermined script. Strategies would collapse into formulas. Existence would become a solved equation rather than a living mystery.

A world without randomness would be perfectly ordered and yet—perfectly lifeless.

This is why the developers chose Natural Simulation instead of direct design.

By allowing complexity to rise from simple rules interacting across vast scales, they created not just a world, but a living uncertainty.

The illusion of randomness grants freedom, fosters resilience, and ensures that each choice the player or character makes, from the local scope, indeed matters in the grand scheme of things. It protects the universe from stagnation and turns existence into an open-ended exploration rather than a predetermined path.

The purpose was never perfection; it was possibility.

* * *

CHAPTER 3

The Crosser

"To believe we are meant to know everything
is the greatest misunderstanding of all.

When we release the burden of needing perfect clarity,
the world itself becomes clearer."

The Copies of the Universe

Henry stood there confused; he could neither understand the dialect the monk and the blue-eyed woman were conversing in, nor make sense of what was happening to him.

The monk took out a bottle from the shelf and prepared a small drink, then handed it to Aloha. She whispered a *mantra* into it and passed it to Henry, asking him to drink.

Aloha explained that it was a neurochemical stimulation drink that would allow them to communicate. Confused but desperate, Henry drank it. Within seconds, he began to understand their dialect—and what the monk was saying.

The monk said slowly, as if choosing each word with care, that they were living in a simulated world and that the entire Universe was simulated as a game.

He added that they knew of three other similar worlds created by Seranagu, a computer genius whom they believed opposed the idea of simulated worlds being created as games. While the other worlds were designed for gameplay, Venna—the world they were in—was the only one where people lived with absolute free will, without any players influencing them.

He explained that there was only one Universe, but several copies of it running in parallel, and in each one of them, a different version of a world like Venna was present.

These worlds were identical in structure because they were all merely copies of the original Universe, created as a base platform by a technological giant.

Seranagu, the monk said, had created these four copies of the world to infiltrate other worlds through a self-evolving system-intrusive code.

The Curse of Knowledge

The monk explained that the people of Venna had known for a long time that they lived in a simulation.

Fear that reality itself could collapse had replaced curiosity, and under a state of endless emergency most people lost motivation and hope, giving rise to prolonged chaos.

Greedy leaders, backed by ruthless enforcers, divided Venna into vast territories and ruled as dictators.

Science was forbidden, except for a few like the monk himself, who studied it through meditation—seeking to understand the simulation and the creation Seranagu had left behind for them. These regimes hunted people like him, forcing them to hide in the Himalayas, which they called the Sohali Mountains.

As the monk described the other three worlds, Henry slowly realized that Earth was not one of them—yet all these worlds sounded exactly like Earth in every description.

When Henry told him that, the monk said that Henry must be from an outside world, a creation not linked to Seranagu's creations.

This, he added with quiet conviction, was precisely what Seranagu had hoped for. Such inter-system crossings were almost impossible and could happen only for individuals with a highly specific genetic makeup.

Several portals existed on each copy of the world, but only those with compatible identity codes could pass through them and such passage would occur only on extremely rare occasions.

Henry, confused and overwhelmed by what he was hearing, asked if there was any way for him to return to Earth.

The monk explained that there were many things Henry still needed to know about crossing between worlds through portals, but it was not the right time for him.

For now, he only needed to know that crossing a portal required a specific information-passage manipulator called a yantra. A yantra could be used only once, and only on a specific time each year when the portal opened.

Henry would have to wait one full year for the next opening. The monk also warned him that one year on Venna did not necessarily equal one year on Earth, as time could move differently across worlds.

The Prophecy

Later, the monk took Henry, Aloha, and a few followers to meet an oracle—an old blind woman living in isolation in the Sohali foothills, just near their small lakeside village.

The oracle immediately sensed the arrival of an inter-system crosser from another world. Moving her hands slowly over Henry's face, as if trying to feel him, she said she had known he would come—a man from Earth—and that she had been waiting for him.

She revealed that a child born out of pure love from Henry and Aloha—the blue-eyed woman endowed with a rare cognitive and genetic anomaly—would possess extraordinary abilities and would one day become the *Mundus Mukta*, the liberator of worlds.

An ancient prophecy in Venna spoke of Mundus Mukta—a saviour destined to emerge when the hidden order of existence could no longer sustain itself.

He would be able to influence emotions and bend probabilities around him and would traverse across worlds at will, as he would carry the signature of the Base Code itself—the code used to simulate the first universe.

* * *

CHAPTER 4
The Base Code

"Evolution is a carefully designed illusion,
a veil that hides the true design.

The purpose lies in allowing life to believe
it is growing on its own."

The Guided Evolution

Before any character was simulated into Earth, the world had already matured into a tapestry of landscapes. Although the entire Universe Framework was naturally simulated through billions of years of dilated time, Earth was shaped under a special protocol known as the Selective Natural Simulation.

The gradual evolution of landmasses, water bodies, aquatic and terrestrial plants, and the generation of adoptable characters was all selectively guided by the same underlying framework—the Base Code.

When applied to the evolution of individual plants and animals, this same framework manifested as a specialized blueprint known as the *Genetic Code*.

Just as the Base Code of the Universe contains the guiding pathways for its gradual evolution into a vast, complex existence, the Genetic Code lays out the plan for the evolution of each individual species of plant or animal within Earth.

The Base Code and the Genetic Code mattered deeply because they held the entire system together.

They provided a guided pathway for growth and variation, ensuring that even within the apparent chaos of natural evolution—driven by its fundamental laws—life unfolded with coherence, continuity, and purpose under a broadly defined cosmic design.

Guided by the Base Code, the oceans emerged first—vast, ancient, and shimmering with potential—cradling the earliest expressions of life.

Over immense stretches of dilated time, continents rose and drifted, shaped by fire, water, and the slow tectonic pulse of the planet.

Only much later did vast forests appear, spreading across the land in deep, gradual waves of greenery.

Deserts appeared where the rains retreated, grasslands unfurled along the open plains, and snowfields formed in the quiet dominion of cold.

Each biome arrived in its own era, unfolding through the shifting rhythms of climate, geology, and the underlying patterns guided by the Base Code framework.

By the time the first characters were naturally simulated into this world, Earth had already woven these epochs together into a single, living masterpiece of creation—a diverse, evolving environment rich with purpose.

Beneath the surface, the underwater realm unfolded as an entire universe of its own.

Sunlight turned into soft silver beams in the shallow water, lighting up corals shaped like quiet, living structures. Hidden trenches, quiet caves, and clouds of plankton added a sense of mystery, while the open sea stretched into a vast space of freedom.

The Emergent Worlds

As the Character Integration Phase began, species were introduced in gradual sequences that, within Earth's dilated time frame, spanned millions of years.

Each new species was guided to emerge through natural transitions from preceding forms, maintaining the continuity and plausibility required by the Base Code, giving the illusion of gradual evolution and avoiding any footprint of abrupt intervention.

The slow, natural addition of new character species allowed ecosystems to reorganize around them and mature with quiet, seamless coherence.

Once a new species had been added, the developers adhered strictly to the principle of Autonomy of Existence.

No character was ever inserted or removed manually. Nature alone determined what endured, flourished, or faded away.

To maintain ecological balance among these newly thriving sets of lively character species, each species was assigned a fixed maximum lifespan—scaled to its size, metabolism, and ecological role.

Plants persisted across long cycles, while animals lived briefer spans to prevent any lineage from overshadowing the fragile equilibrium.

While the generation of every new species was guided by the Base Code and carried forward by the Genetic Code, their survival was shaped by three fundamental intrinsic impulses: the will to *survive*, the capacity to *grow*, and the drive to *reproduce*.

These were known as the *Basic Instincts*.

From these simple directives, complex patterns emerged on their own. Characters dispersed across the oceans, settled where resources were plentiful, and became prey where danger pressed upon them.

Populations rose and fell, territories shifted, and entire lineages appeared and vanished—all as natural expressions of a world governed by a handful of fundamental rules rather than direct intervention.

The Water Worlds

The first official gameplay released within Earth was called Water World. Here, players could adopt one of the aquatic characters available for adoption.

They could then gently shape the surroundings—subtly adjusting currents, influencing light gradients, or modulating nutrient flows.

Characters responded according to their instincts; they could follow these cues or ignore them entirely, acting from their own internal logic guided by their three Basic Instincts.

This interplay between suggestion and autonomy became the heart of the game experience.

The idea was simple yet profound: players could influence life, but never completely control it.

This gave the gameplay an extraordinary challenge—how does one strategize toward a goal within a chaotic storm of probabilities and free will, when full control over one's characters is never possible?

And how do two individuals of free will—the player and the character—communicate and connect through a medium of only instincts and possibilities, and how effectively can the player assess and anticipate the future of their character within the chaos of probabilities and choices?

Neither the player nor the character could foresee with accuracy what might unfold.

Any outcome following a player's input might arise directly from their influence—or might simply be the environment expressing its own natural complexity, leaving players unable to know with certainty whether a favourable condition was shaped by their guidance or by the world acting entirely on its own.

For characters, this ambiguity was existence itself: a continual test of resilience, adaptation, and instinct.

When a character survived long enough to grow, thrive, and reproduce, the player earned qualia points—a measure of emotional resonance reflecting the depth of their influence within this unpredictable, awe-filled marine world.

Water World became more than a game; it was a living demonstration of emergence and intention, revealing the delicate balance between guidance and independence.

It portrayed a universe where beauty and risk, autonomy and design, existed side by side.

Within that balance lay its inherent wonder—the most challenging and yet most magnificent aspect of existence, and a subtle expression of the elegance of Natural Simulation.

* * *

CHAPTER 5
The World of Suffering

"In the depths of despair, when hope feels lost
and anguish reaches its peak,

And when every heart stands ready to surrender,
that is when the liberator arises."

Between Family and Fate

Henry still could not believe that he was in another world other than Earth or that his entire existence was part of a grand simulated game.

The oracle continued that the child born out of him and Aloha, when he turned seventeen, would reveal the truth and liberate not just Venna, but thousands of worlds like Venna and Earth—from the simulation itself.

Henry, in a tone of disbelief, told the oracle that he had a wife and two children waiting for him, and that he could not help fight their war, as he needed to go back home.

He told her that he was just an ordinary man who, aside from fixing and driving cars, possessed no special skills or abilities.

He insisted that it was all a misunderstanding and that he had landed among a primitive people in the Himalayas with no knowledge of real science.

He also told her that he did not believe they lived in a simulation, because everything felt too real.

He begged them to release him so that he could return to his family.

The Weight of Venna's Past

Seeing that Henry was still in denial, the monk drew a yantra on the floor and told Henry to sit with him, take his hand, and imagine that they—he and the monk—were one.

Reluctantly, when Henry did, a spark of light flashed between their hands and from the yantra, and Henry suddenly went into a trance.

He saw the entire evolution of Venna flash in sequence through his mind.

He witnessed battles—small and large—fought across its world, people suffering under cruel rulers, and countless massacres, with women and children perishing in merciless chaos.

He also saw that Aloha's mother had been killed when she was just four years old.

The world was too dark and too dangerous.

Henry slowly opened his eyes.

The Paradox of Creation

The monk told him that this was the history of Venna, transferred from his mind to Henry's through meditation.

Meditation, the monk explained, is the ultimate art for accessing the hidden layers of consciousness.

And since everything, including our bodies and all matter in the Universe, is just information, an ability to access this information through the hidden layers of consciousness can show one the ultimate truth about reality itself.

He continued to explain that everything we see, hear, feel, or sense is information that our brains perceive in a three-dimensional construct.

All of us are packets of information interacting with other packets, and the entire Universe is a game.

The Universe is the base framework, and Earth and other worlds like Venna are instances—copies of a game environment—plugged into the core Universal Framework.

These instances are not meant to interact with each other, but Seranagu wanted to break the simulation. He created these four copies of the world, including Venna, and embedded a system-inflicting virus code in the hope that one day a unique gene sequence would emerge that could transcend worlds and liberate all people from all instances of the Universe.

The irony, the monk continued, was that Seranagu created a world of suffering to free all the other worlds from suffering.

Henry asked in confusion why, if everything was a simulation, and if nothing was real, people suffered so much.

The monk told him that even if they were only information projected onto a simulated world, to the mind it was real.

Pain was real, and death was real and painful; and no one wanted to die.

As Henry slowly began to believe some of what the monk was telling him, the monk said that Henry still needed to learn the truth about inter-system crossing.

He also said that he could promise to help Henry return to Earth, but only after the portal opened again, one year from then.

There was no other choice but to stay with them and try to stay alive.

* * *

CHAPTER 6
Natural Simulation

"A perfect creation is one that forgets it is a creation, and begins to believe it is the creator itself.

When the rules are unseen, when interactions flow without interference, the world awakens."

The Hollow World

How could everything even feel so real?

If everything we see, perceive, or feel is just a construct of our consciousness, then what is this consciousness?

What are we?

It does seem true, doesn't it—that we and all our senses are made only of information and signals.

If we look at an atom, it is composed largely of fields rather than solid structure—almost empty, almost hollow.

These atoms, stacked one upon another, form us and all matter in the Universe.

We are, in essence, hollow objects.

Then how do we feel so real?

And if we are nothing more than a hologram, where does our consciousness come from?

The Limits of Design

When the idea of simulating the Universe was conceived, the purpose was not to simulate matter, stars, planets, or galaxies. Because even if we simulated them, if we could not simulate consciousness into them to feel the existence of it all, there would be no existence itself.

In essence, we are not real solid objects. It is the sense of consciousness that makes existence real.

Without consciousness, there is no existence at all.

So, how do we go about creating consciousness?

The answer was Natural Simulation.

Here, we do not create. We let something emerge on its own by dilating local time, giving it billions of years of its own to form itself.

It was essential because it allowed the Universe to evolve in a way that felt organic, spontaneous, and unpredictable.

By letting matter interact naturally under only a minimal set of pre-defined rules, rather than forcing every outcome, the simulation could generate true randomness, subtle effects of probability, and cascading consequences from small variations.

It ensured diversity in forms and behaviors, and allowed unexpected interactions to occur—where chaos could dance within order, and complexity could bloom from simplicity, something no algorithm could fully foresee.

Without Natural Simulation, every event would be predetermined, every life predictable, and the Universe would lose the depth, richness, and mystery that made it capable of hosting dynamic, interactive characters.

The First Building Block

It all began with the very first simulation of an atom. Without this single breakthrough, nothing that followed would ever have been possible. The simulated atom became the foundational building block of Natural Simulation—a tiny unit of structured illusion upon which the entire Universe Framework would be constructed.

Each simulated atom was a tiny spark of structured possibility—existing only within the Universe, yet behaving as if it were real, and forming the foundation for everything that would emerge.

It only formed a defined structure when interacting with something else—a method designed to save processing power while mimicking the unpredictability of natural interactions.

Simulated atoms possess no actual mass or shape, but they behave as if they do when observed or engaged. Each atom is simply a system-level information package generated by algorithmic code and projected into the Universe Framework.

While the Universe runs on a common server, several instances of the Earth can run simultaneously, each hosting different versions of the games developed by different groups of developers.

They call this a Modular Simulation Framework. It works like creating copies of Earth as plugins to the Universe—each instance plugs into the same universal engine, accessing the same core rules and systems without interfering with one another.

Simulating the Universe in real time would have taken years, so the developers introduced a *Time Dilation* Protocol, accelerating Universe development by millions of times. Depending on its dilation setting, one hour of real time could stretch into millions or even billions of years inside the simulation.

The Earth game, however, had a different time dilation setting, progressing much slower to suit the patience of its players. Each instance of Earth could even have its own unique time dilation parameters.

As simulated matter interacted under a fixed set of fundamental laws—also known as the *Prime Directives*—it clustered to form stars, planets, and a variety of other objects, many of which the developers didn't even have names for. Although this process appeared to span billions of years from within the Universe, in real time it took only a couple of hours for the Universe to fully load when first booted on the master server.

The Earth Environment

The pre-loaded Earth Environment, launched alongside the Universe Framework, followed the same principles of Natural Simulation.

Earth was naturally simulated in three major phases according to Universe time. First came the Accretion Phase, where matter interacted naturally to form the base world, shaping vast oceans, mountains, plains, networks of rivers, and ice-covered regions.

Next was the Emergence Phase, in which life began to take hold: single-celled organisms naturally evolved into more complex forms capable of converting solar energy into stored energy, establishing a self-sustaining environment and preserving the core principle of Autonomy of Existence.

Finally, the Character Integration Phase brought millions of species into existence, each now able to interact with one another and with players.

Earth became vibrant and alive, teeming with creatures on land and in water, all part of a larger interconnected system designed for dynamic interaction.

The first version of the Earth Environment was launched with only one game, called Water World, where players could adopt different aquatic predator animals like sharks and craft situations for their characters to prey on smaller creatures or rival predators.

Water-based ecosystems were chosen first, because they required far fewer computational variables than land environments, making them ideal for early testing and gameplay.

Later updates expanded the environment with more species, including land animals and mega-predators like the dinosaurs, gradually increasing the complexity and strategic depth of the game.

The Curious Character

The introduction of fully conscious *Humans* came much later, after intense debate over morality, free will, and the ethical implications of allowing players to influence beings capable of thought and reflection.

Humans were eventually added to the list of characters available for gameplay, with carefully calibrated parameters that granted them creativity, choice, and consequence—yet still kept them operating within the rules of the Universe Framework.

This transformed the simulation into its most intricate gameplay stage, where every interaction, decision, and relationship became a layer of strategy.

Players could now engage with characters that were not only alive in form but alive in thought, capable of shaping their own destinies while participating in a larger, interconnected game of endless possibilities.

* * *

CHAPTER 7
The Burden of Truth

"Not every truth offers relief,
and not every revelation heals.

Sometimes, ignorance offers more shelter than understanding."

The Pain of Memory

That night, Henry could not sleep well, his mind heavy with unresolved thoughts.

On one side, Henry still couldn't fully believe what the monk had told him. On the other, his mind was consumed by the thought that his wife and children must be devastated by his disappearance.

He remembered his wife showing him pictures of colorful sea fishes on her cellphone, smiling and leaning on him as she scrolled. He remembered the two kids casually fighting inside the tent over a video game the night before the storm came.

The memories tightened his chest.

It was past midnight, with only a little time left before sunrise. Henry slowly looked around and there was no one awake.

Quietly, he rose and slipped out of the hut, careful not to make a sound. There were no lights anywhere, but the moon shone brightly, casting pale silver over the mountains. In its glow, Henry could see the narrow trails leading away from the lakeside—the same path they had taken when they first arrived.

He quickly but quietly followed it.

Through a winding trail between small, rocky hills, he reached the place where the campsite was supposed to be.

But, there was nothing.

No caravans, no tents, no public toilets, no fireplaces—nothing.

"This can't be true," he whispered to himself, his voice trembling.

He remembered there was a small town just beyond the campsite—shops, local restaurants, lights. He ran toward where it should have been.

But again, there was nothing.

Henry kept walking, driven by desperation, hoping to find at least one person—someone who could explain whether what was happening to him was real.

As he moved through the darkness, he noticed a small fire burning in the distance.

Hope surged through him.

He ran toward it and reached a rough clearing with a few small hut-like tents. He called out softly, asking if anyone was there.

Suddenly, a few rough men grabbed him from behind.

Before he could react, a man stepped in front of him, holding a blade that looked like a machete. The men moved fast, efficient, ruthless.

They were about to kill him.

Just then, chaos erupted.

A brief, violent struggle broke out as Aloha and several men from the lakeside village rushed in, attacking Henry's captors. The fight was short but brutal.

When it ended, they took Henry back toward the lake.

The Man from Rigga

As they walked back towards the village, Aloha spoke softly. She told Henry she understood how hard it was for him to believe the monk.

She explained that many years ago, another crosser had arrived—someone from a world called Rigga, one of the four creations of Seranagu. Like Henry, the man had refused to believe he had crossed into another world. He thought the monk and the villagers were primitive hill tribes trying to deceive him.

Henry looked at her with curiosity and asked what happened to that man.

Aloha's expression darkened.

"He left," she said. "And we did not try to stop him."

She paused before adding, "Anyone as naïve as he would not have survived even a day in Venna."

She then added that the monk knew many things that they do not, and if he wants to stay alive and return to his wife and children, he must trust the monk.

Aloha sounded calm, but Henry could tell it was a calm born out of some past loss.

When they got back to the village, it was already morning, the monk was quietly seated in meditation. Henry slowly got near him and sat quietly next to the monk. He looked at the thin air, grief filling his eyes, and after a pause, he softly said, "This cannot be the truth."

The monk slowly opened his eyes and looked at Henry. He then stood and walked toward the wide open door facing the garden. Henry followed him.

He looked at a few kids playing by the small pond when Henry, standing by his side, asked, "How can this not be real? How can this be a game?"

The Veda Mandala

The monk looked at Henry and said, "There is a place called *Veda Mandala*—the cave of knowing, eleven miles uphill from the village."

He then added, "You will get answers to some of your questions there."

When Henry asked what kind of place it was, the monk explained that it was a cave where all the senses would be suppressed, allowing one to temporarily access consciousness at its fullest potential—a place where one would feel nothing, yet see everything.

The monk added that the cave had appeared from nowhere several years ago, and no one knew how it came to exist.

Perhaps, he said quietly, it was something designed to emerge by the Creator itself—for moments when one is lost in darkness and wants to seek the truth.

In a consoling tone, the monk then said, "If you really want to know the truth, I will take you there tomorrow. Today, you must take rest."

Later that evening, as Henry lay awake beneath the unfamiliar sky, his thoughts refused to settle. The monk's words echoed in his mind, colliding with memories of his world that still felt painfully real.

If worlds could be built, and if all that was seen existed as a game, then the truth he sought was far larger than his own fate.

How did something as immense and complex as the Universe come to be a creation? And if all of this was a game, how had it all begun?

Whatever answers awaited him in Veda Mandala, Henry did not even know if he was ready for them.

* * *

CHAPTER 8

Evolution of the Game

"We must set aside the good
to create space for what could be extraordinary.

Progress emerges when we dare to disrupt what feels settled."

The Birth of Adoption

In Water World, the first version of the game launched with the release of the Earth, players could adopt aquatic creatures—predators and prey alike—and interact with their surroundings in subtle ways.

Players could slightly adjust currents, influence light, etc., using the inbuilt Situation Engine. The player could also inject the characters with simple emotions like hunger, fear, etc., using the Emotion Engine.

These were not acts of direct control but gentle guidance, respecting the Autonomy of Existence.

The challenge emerged naturally: survival required reading delicate signals – both from the surroundings and from injections, processing them through the lens of their own past experience, predicting probabilities, and adapting to a constantly shifting environment shaped both by fundamental laws and by the environmental influence of other players.

Even the simplest fish or shark became a microcosm of strategy, instinct, and emergent interaction.

Characters in Water World emerged with only a handful of emotions like hunger, fear, aggression, and attraction. Early forms of instinct and curiosity were present in some species, marking the first emergence of adaptive behavior.

Emotions, as adaptive responses to uncertainty and environmental randomness, require millions of years of dilated evolutionary time to mature. They never appear fully formed; they crystallize slowly, layer by layer, as life learns to survive, predict, and adapt within an unpredictable world.

The Art of Subtle Influence

Once a player adopted a character, they could induce emotions to guide its strategic path—supporting survival, growth, and combat to accumulate qualia points.

Players could also use the Situation Engine to shape environmental scenarios that helped their character reach key strategic milestones. Unlike the Emotion Engine, the Situation Engine was constrained by the fundamental rules of the environment; deployable scenarios appeared only when conditions allowed, and using them required a significantly higher expenditure of qualia points.

Equipped with these two engines, players were free to craft strategies, deploy plans, and guide their characters toward game plan milestones, unlocking more advanced engine features as they progressed.

The first release of the Universe was built primarily to demonstrate that something of this magnitude could be simulated at all.

From the beginning, developers hinted at a far more advanced Emotion Engine that would unfold as the natural simulation deepened and grew in complexity.

The Limits of Predatory Dcsign

The next major upgrade arrived when land animals became ready for adoption. It marked the epitome of direct-combat gameplay, with its most significant phase being the era of *Dinosaurs*—the ultimate predators a player could adopt after accumulating enough qualia points.

Several new emotions were added to the Emotion Engine: territoriality, dominance and submission, parental protective instinct, and rivalry, among others.

Early versions of social bonding and sexual competition also appeared with this phase of upgrades.

These new sets of emotions enabled richer strategies and higher-stakes survival, dramatically enhancing the game's depth and challenge.

It became one of the most spectacular eras of gameplay in the Universe Game World.

But as refined as the gameplay had become, a critical concern emerged—ecological stagnation.

Within several million years of dilated time inside the Univcrsc, Dinosaurs dominated nearly every strategic terrestrial niche. Their strength, size, and hyper-efficiency caused evolution to plateau, leaving little room for new emotional or cognitive pathways to arise.

This became a serious issue the developers needed to address.

The Correction Patch

After several rounds of debate and a final consensus, the developers deployed a major update called the Environmental Correction Patch—a drastic situational reset intended to reopen the evolutionary path and allow more complex emotional and cognitive engines to develop.

Within the gaming community, this event became known as the *Extinction Update*, and many players were deeply vocal against it.

Some felt it was unfair to the Dinosaurs and to life itself; others argued the developers had interfered too heavily with the autonomy of the Natural Simulation.

But nevertheless, looking back at it from the present, it is widely acknowledged to have been the right decision.

Had Dinosaurs continued to dominate the Earth, the Emotion Engine would never have matured beyond its early forms in the same time span.

Large-brain characters would not have emerged so soon, and the strategic consciousness that defined the Human Phase would have been significantly delayed.

The next few phases of the game continued to be dominated by terrestrial characters and land-based strategies, but the most transformative update arrived when Humans were announced to be ready for adoption.

The Birth of Conscious Combats

The most notable change accompanying the Human update was the shift in gameplay from pure survival, combat, and predator mode to a more complex structure of survival and organized combat gameplay.

The Human Era, however, did not arrive suddenly. It emerged as the natural consequence of every phase before it: the fluid instincts of fish, the toughness of reptiles, the warmth of mammals, and the ingenuity of apes.

For the first time, characters were not merely surviving within the system; they were capable of reflecting on it.

Humans became strategists themselves, able to influence their environment and be shaped by it in return. This phase introduced unprecedented volatility, creativity, danger, cooperation, and conflict.

Every previous stage had been challenging, but the Human Era brought a new kind of complexity: a consciousness capable of questioning itself.

At the launch of the Human Phase, the gameplay remained primarily strategic and combat-driven, much like the other previous upgrades of Earth.

While Human combats on Earth began with small-scale fights for survival, it gradually evolved toward complex strategies involving thousands—and eventually millions—of characters.

Players drove characters to form alliances, manipulate environments, establish tribes and early kingdoms, and launch coordinated attacks to seize land and resources.

These large-scale wars yielded enormous amounts of qualia points.

Some players and their characters built massive empires, orchestrating conflicts that reshaped entire geopolitical landscapes.

The game thrived in excitement, challenge, and spectacle, but the consequences were severe.

From conflicts once limited to territorial boundaries, strategic warfare began to grow in size, frequency, and impact.

The Cognition Patch

Within a matter of a few thousand years in Earth's timeline, massive conflicts began to unfold, their effects reaching far and wide.

These large-scale confrontations terminated characters in staggering numbers, sounding alarms among developers and critics alike.

A growing debate emerged between players and developers about the morality of mass-scale combat and the ethical boundaries of a game simulation designed for evolution—not endless destruction.

The final blow came when a series of extremely devastating worldwide strategic wars began to take shape, gradually leading to the termination of nearly five percent of the entire Human character population.

After extensive discussion and a final consensus, a patch known as the *Cognition Patch* was introduced into the game to accelerate the emergence of social awareness and participatory governance among characters, gradually reshaping how societies formed, cooperated, and evolved on Earth.

The developers also released a major Qualia Reward Update that drastically reduced rewards for mass warfare and large-scale annihilation, shifting the incentive structure away from combat-centric strategies.

Higher qualia points were now awarded to players who fostered social development, improved their characters' quality of life, and designed complex cooperative systems.

This update fundamentally reshaped the game, ushering in a new era of responsible, evolution-aligned gameplay—a paradigm shift soon referred to among players as the Civilization Shift.

The evolution of the game called Universe was never a straight path.

It was a tapestry woven from countless interactions, failures, adaptations, and emergent strategies.

From water to land, from scales to fur to thought, each phase was not a replacement but a refinement.

Through these phases, the simulation expanded layer by layer, preparing itself for characters capable of deeper reflection, choice, and the subtle orchestration of their own destinies.

* * *

CHAPTER 9
The Cave of Knowing

"We want to know everything before its time.

Yet it is the unknown that gives us the courage to move forward and let life unfold."

A Cave from Another World

The next morning, Henry and the monk, along with a few men from the village, took the mountain trail leading toward Veda Mandala—the Cave of Knowing.

The entrance to the cave was small, almost indistinguishable from the other cracks in the surrounding stones. It allowed only one person to enter at a time, with water drops slowly dripping from thin fissures in the ceiling. After passing through a long, zigzag passage of dark, narrow tunnels, the path suddenly widened.

The cave passage emerged into a vast cavern—nearly three storeys high.

The walls were carved with intricate, futuristic designs, embedded with dark grey, metallic-like minerals.

Nothing about it felt natural. Instead, the cave looked as though it had been shaped with extreme precision, as if carved by a massive machine rather than by time itself.

Dim rays of light fell from above and from six distinct directions. At the centre stood a large hexagonal plate, made of a metallic-looking material, carved with fine lines and symbols resembling ancient script.

All six rays from different directions, along with a straight beam descending from the ceiling, converged precisely at the centre of the hexagonal plate.

The sight was mesmerizing—as if energy from the entire Universe was being drawn into a single point inside this magnificent cave.

The monk asked Henry to sit with him at the center of the plate.

Henry asked if this was like the time the monk had used the yantra to show him the history of Venna.

"That was about me," the monk replied. "This is about you."

When they were both seated, he told Henry to close his eyes and let go of all thoughts, feelings, and emotions.

The monk softly told Henry to think of the Universe as a living soul, and to understand that he himself was also the Universe. Though they existed in different forms, he and the Universe were one.

"You just have to believe it and the energy of Veda Mandala," the monk said softly, "will do the rest."

The monk then slowly began to recite a mantra in a rhythm that sounded like a steady pulse, rising and falling like breath itself, and the rhythm echoed as if the cave were listening and repeating it in perfect resonance.

The Quiet Revelation

When Henry opened his eyes, a day had already passed, and it was morning again.

Yet he had felt no passage of time at all. It was as if time itself had paused to reveal the truth to him.

Something inside Henry had changed.

His anxious mind seemed to have left him, replaced by calmness, as though the weight he had been carrying no longer needed to be held.

The monk, now standing beside him, gently placed a hand on Henry's shoulder.

"Many years ago, I saw my purpose when I sat here for fourteen days," the monk said in a calm tone.

"And one of those purposes was to bring you here, when the time came."

During his sixteen-hour-long meditative state, Henry's consciousness expanded, allowing him to see and feel things from perspectives no one had ever imagined.

He saw the vastness of the Universe, but from a scope much larger than himself. He realized that the creators did not want anyone to suffer. They never meant any harm.

Yet people suffered, people died before their time, and loved ones got separated. Henry understood that all of this was part of a system gradually moving toward a greater plan.

Each one of us is given a choice at every moment of our lives, and we choose what we believe is best from that vantage point.

And it is not fair to judge the decisions of our past with the information we have now.

We are here to simply play our part, experience life through our choices, and not to understand it, because we were never meant to understand it all.

Henry's Purpose

Henry's consciousness travelled far and deep. He saw worlds; he saw people, buildings, advanced technologies, and people laughing, running, crying, and dying.

He witnessed events: wars beginning and wars ending, revolutions rising, civilizations flourishing. He saw Veda Mandala, saw Aloha, children playing, and people rejoicing.

And through all these seemingly unrelated visions, his consciousness was slowly searching for its own identity and meaning.

Henry's consciousness then went back to Earth.

He could see his wife and his children and feel them. It was as if he was replaying events in real time, feeling everything as if they were happening in that moment.

He saw them at the campsite.

He saw himself lost during the storm. He saw his wife and children crying, desperately searching for him.

He felt emotions rise and fall within him as he saw and felt his wife and children in flesh, as if everything were happening in that very moment, and he stood at the center of it all.

But then, as his emotions settled, his visions became clearer, and he saw himself playing with his children back home, with his beloved wife beside him.

He could feel them all, and he knew it was real.

Although many of the visions he saw did not fully make sense, Henry now knew one thing for certain—when all of this was over, he would return home to his wife and children and live a happy life once again.

He had seen his future with them through his visions, and to him, it felt real and alive. It was only a matter of time, and he could truly feel it now.

Sensing the confusion in Henry's mind, the monk said, "I know many things must still be unclear. But your consciousness now holds it all; gradually, but surely, it will reveal itself when the time is right for you."

"And you will understand what your true purpose is," he added in a consoling tone.

"It is often important for us to give time for the Universe to reveal itself," the monk continued. "We all want to know everything before its time, but the irony is that if we knew everything, we wouldn't do what we are meant to do for the future to unfold."

On one hand, it was consoling for Henry to see himself returning home in the future; on the other, he wondered what the monk truly meant when he said the Universe would reveal his purpose in time.

And if he was meant to return to Earth, what would that mean for the prophecy of Mundus Mukta, the prophecy the oracle and the monk guarded so closely?

And what would that mean for Aloha?

* * *

CHAPTER 10
The Human Character

"Be humble enough to listen to your heart,
for it often knows the truth long before the mind does.

True strength is not the absence of influence,
but clarity of choice within it."

The Conscious Characters

Humans are a deeply fascinating set of characters.

Human characters have emotions almost fully developed, and they can reason.

They can ask questions, doubt what they are told, and imagine possibilities beyond what they see. They are capable of love, sacrifice, fear, ambition, and regret—sometimes feeling them all at once.

They can reflect on their past, anticipate their future, and make choices that are not driven purely by the three Basic Instincts—survival, growth, or reproduction.

Unlike earlier character sets, Humans do not just react to the world—they interpret it, reshape it, and sometimes even challenge the very rules that govern it.

They can even devise, optimize, and deploy strategies, much like the players themselves.

But what do the players do with such a complicated character set?

Adoption and Influence

In the Earth Environment of the Universe Game, a player can adopt a character based on their ranks and ratings by paying a premium.

They may also choose to adopt a free character—usually a child character—and help it grow through the ranks.

Characters receive their ranks and ratings based on their resonance with previous players, as well as with the Emotion and Situation Engine injections.

Many players prefer to adopt free child characters, nurturing and developing them over time while earning consistent qualia points.

A player can modulate the right amount of emotional makeup to guide the character, helping it learn, adapt, and progress through society, all while accumulating qualia points themselves.

Some players with substantial qualia reserves may choose to adopt highly rated characters with superior rankings.

These players engage in high-stakes strategies that influence unexpectedly large numbers of characters within the game world, involving massive amounts of qualia points.

Regardless of whether a player adopts a free child character or pays a premium for one with superior ratings, the fundamental challenge remains the same: how do you navigate your character through a world of interconnected beings—each with their own goals, instincts, influences, and hidden pressures—while steering it toward a greater purpose or shaping it into something more impactful?

The Player's Problem

Because time is dilated inside the game world, players cannot monitor their characters moment by moment.

Instead, they set goals, calibrate the emotional makeup of their characters to match their game plan, and allow them to navigate on their own—while monitoring, from time to time, the overall progress and the character's alignment with the larger game plan.

As characters gradually mature, they naturally develop intuitive free will—shaped by experiences, emotional fluctuations, and the complexities of their social interactions, something unique to each character in the game.

Meanwhile, players can inject emotions from time to time or deploy situational cues, subtly nudging the character toward intended goals or aligning the character's internal motivations with their overarching strategies.

The players must assess whether the character they adopt will resonate strongly enough with the qualia they spend to generate emotions through the Emotion Engine, and whether the character can correctly interpret the Situation Engine cues intended to move the game plan forward.

Their overarching goal is to shape the character so that it aligns closely with their strategy, responds positively to emotional injections, and remains receptive to the situational cues arranged around them.

The ultimate dream is for the character to resonate so perfectly that it moves in complete harmony with the player's intent.

Yet achieving such seamless alignment is nearly impossible—spoken of in legends, but rarely witnessed in the Universe Game.

The Character's Problem

For the characters, the challenge is equally intricate. For them, life itself is a challenge—an ongoing internal negotiation between right and wrong, fear and ambition, compassion and aggression.

Each character, once born into the game—whether guided by a player or not—must continuously make choices under uncertainty, never knowing which emotional impulse is natural and which has been nudged by a player.

They fight through shifting emotional currents, making decisions based on anticipation alone, never fully aware of what will ultimately unfold.

When a player finds that a character is no longer resonating with their expectations or aligning with their strategic aims, they may choose to release that character and adopt a new one.

Characters released in this way are known as *Abandoned Characters.*

Once released or abandoned, they return to the general pool of available characters, awaiting adoption by other players.

While many players prefer to begin by adopting child characters—an accessible and cost-free entry into the game—the ultimate aim of every player is to maximize strategic impact inside the game through their characters.

In doing so, these players play a significant role in shaping and reshaping the world within the Earth environment.

* * *

CHAPTER 11
Guardians of Mundus Mukta

"We all must endure suffering, for it is only through pain that we come to understand the true value of liberation.

What is never lost is never truly found."

The Aggressors

As they walked back toward the village from Veda Mandala, Henry, the monk, and the village men slowed when they heard hostile noises and noticed movement ahead.

From a distance, they noticed more than forty men gathered around the huts. Some were on horseback, circling like wolves. Even from far away, Henry could feel the danger in them—hard faces and loud, aggressive voices.

The monk quickly pulled everyone toward a huge rock along the trail on the hillside.

"Hide," he whispered.

They crouched behind the stone, peeking out.

The village looked damaged. A few huts had been broken into. Some roofs were torn, and the ground was trampled. The loose wooden pole fences around the plantations were kicked down and scattered, and young plants lay crushed under boots and hooves.

Henry's stomach turned when he saw two village men on the ground, bruised and barely moving, while others stood back helplessly.

Near the open village ground in front of the huts, Aloha and a few women stood close together, tense and silent. Their faces were tight with fear, but they tried not to show it.

The aggressors were spread out in front of them, blocking the way, making the air feel heavy.

Then one man, clearly important, wearing a rough woollen shawl thrown loosely over his shoulder, stepped sharply forward toward them.

He walked straight toward Aloha and began speaking harshly. He jabbed a finger in her direction and waved his hand in a sharp, commanding motion, like he was giving orders and warnings at the same time.

Aloha's Father

Henry's body moved before his mind did. He started to stand.

"We should go," he whispered. "He'll hurt her."

The monk lifted a hand and pressed it gently against Henry's chest, stopping him.

"No," the monk said softly. "He won't."

Henry stared at him, confused and angry. "How can you be so sure?"

The monk didn't look away from the scene. His voice stayed calm.

"Because," he said, "that's her father."

For a moment, his breath caught in his throat as he tried to make sense of a situation that now seemed more complicated than it first appeared.

Henry and the monk stayed hidden behind the rock and kept watching.

They could hear raised voices and angry sounds drifting through the air, but the words were unclear. Still, it was obvious the man was not saying anything kind to Aloha.

The tension hung heavy, like something bad was about to happen at any moment.

After a while, the man gave a final loud shout. Then he turned away. His men followed him, leaving the village roughly, kicking dirt, shouting, and riding off on their horses, as if they wanted to leave fear behind them.

That evening, as the sun dipped behind the mountains, the village people gathered with the monk, Henry, and Aloha. They sat together quietly, trying to understand what the visit of the aggressors meant and what danger it had brought with it.

The man who visited them was a tribal Chief, feared across the region. He controlled a large part of the land around Aloha's village along the foothills with the help of his ruthless followers, ruling through fear and force.

He worked directly under one of the Dictators who ruled a large subcontinent of Venna.

Aloha's Mother

Aloha's mother belonged to a small semi-nomadic tribe called the Saimu tribe, the same tribe as the people of the village. They moved often along the Sohali foothills, living simple lives as shepherds, raising sheep and goats.

Her mother, when she was young, was known for her beauty in the village. She was cheerful and full of life.

But it was that very beauty that turned her cheerful life into one of fear and sorrow.

When she was only fourteen, the Chief saw her one day while she was herding goats along a hill trail as he passed through. He seized her and took her away by force, without mercy and without choice.

Years later, when Aloha was just four years old, her mother found the courage to stand against his cruelty. And for that, in a fateful confrontation, the Chief killed her.

After her mother's death, Aloha's grandmother went to the Chief and begged him to let the child live with her among the village people.

When her grandmother died a few years later from a winter illness, Aloha was taken in by the village women.

From then on, she grew up around the lake, moving with the nomadic people of the village, watched over by the women—and quietly guided and protected by the monk, who became the closest thing she had to family.

Now that Aloha had grown into a young, beautiful woman, the Chief, as a token of loyalty, wanted to offer her to the Dictator, to be taken as one of his wives.

This was not the first time he had come to express this demand, but this time he left a clear, irrevocable ultimatum.

He demanded that she come to him willingly within the next seven days, or he swore he would burn down the village and kill her with his own hands.

That was the message the chief left, and it fell over the village like a dark shadow.

"Will he really kill her?" Henry asked the monk, his voice low and shaken.

"The Chief is a dangerous man," the monk replied after a moment of pause. "But I have seen the way he looks at her. He does not have the heart to kill her."

He turned to look at Henry and continued. "But it is too great a risk to take," he said. "You must take her to *Washida.* It is the only place that would protect her and the village people."

The Story of Washida

Washida, the land of the Washis, is a place even the Chiefs and Dictators would rarely dare to enter.

It lies a few hundred miles east along the foothills of the Sohali Mountains. It is a vast, living ocean of towering evergreen trees that stretches for hundreds of miles in every direction. The forest is deep, dense, and dark, swallowing sound and light as one moves farther inside.

The Washis are considered a sacred tribe, scattered sparsely across the forest. They live in small clusters deep within the thick woods, hidden from the outside world.

They are feared by many and are extremely hostile toward outsiders, masters of guerrilla warfare and known especially for their deadly poisoned arrows.

Yet among themselves, they are deeply disciplined and devoted, fiercely protective of their families and people, and are known for their profound tradition of meditation practice.

An old tale says that the Washis do not truly belong to this world.

Long ago, they lived alongside the Creators themselves.

But their ancestors once broke a promise they had made to the Creators, and as a path toward redemption, the Washis were sent to live as humans for five thousand years deep inside the Washida Forest—a place filled with deadly predators and dangers they could never fully fathom.

When the five thousand years came to an end, the Creators refused to take them back. Instead, they gave the Washis one final trial.

The Creators told them that when the time came, a child of the Creators would be born into their world.

The Washis would have to protect, nurture, and raise this child for seventeen years, until he was ready to free them from their transgression and long suffering, and liberate them to become one with the Creators once again.

The story says that this child would be known as Mundus Mukta—the Liberator of Worlds.

* * *

CHAPTER 12
The Path Through Maya

"When awareness sharpens and intuition leads,
confusion settles into clarity and purpose.

Only then does one align with
the subtle intelligence shaping existence."

The World of Illusion

Is there a way to influence reality?

Are our intuitions a guide to beating this game?

How do we move forward and play our role in the grand scheme of things?

Ancient philosophy suggests that our ancestors may have understood far more about our origins and purpose than we often give them credit for.

Ancient Indian scriptures, for instance, tell us that we are not merely human beings searching for meaning—we are divine beings temporarily experiencing life as humans.

Once our purpose is fulfilled, they say, we, as consciousness, return to the Creator and merge back into the source from which we came.

They describe this world as *Maya*—an illusion, a dream, a beautifully crafted projection that hides the ultimate reality beneath its shifting surface.

Buddhism speaks of a deeper truth behind appearances. Ancient Greek philosophers questioned the nature of reality and the reliability of perception.

Taoist thinkers in ancient China described the world as a flowing pattern of forces rather than a fixed, solid structure.

Across cultures and centuries, the message was remarkably similar: we live inside a constructed reality, a layered experience, beneath which lies a higher truth.

But who constructed it?

And why?

And what happened to these philosophies?

Why did we gradually drift away from these ideas that once guided cultures and civilizations?

Did someone want us to stop exploring them?

Were we distracted intentionally, gently nudged—perhaps by the guided path of the Base Code—toward ambition, technology, industry, and material progress?

Or is it simply that we are in a vast puzzle game, and we chose this path among many possibilities—and we will not know whether it is the right one until we reach a dead end?

Or will every path we take converge toward the same thing: the truth that we are, in fact, inside a constructed reality, a simulated game.

But even knowing this truth still leaves us with a deeper question: how are we meant to live inside a simulated game?

The Path to the Truth

Apparently, there are four paths through which we, as characters, can resonate more clearly with the guiding forces within the game: Meditation, Devotion, Discipline, and Selflessness.

Meditation helps the character watch their own thoughts and feelings. Over time, it allows them to notice small signals, understand what is natural and what is guided, and respond calmly instead of reacting to every emotion.

It reduces suffering by helping the character see that not everything is meant to unfold according to their expectations, and that not everything can be controlled.

It helps them make wiser choices and avoid impulsive actions that interfere with their progress.

Devotion opens up the character's heart and strengthens their inner alignment with whatever guiding force they feel, whether they understand it or not.

A devoted character becomes more emotionally steady, more receptive, and more trusting of the subtle impulses that shape their choices.

They fight their emotions less and find it easier to follow the quiet pull of intuition, moving in a direction that feels meaningful—even without knowing who or what may be guiding them. This allows them to fall into harmony with the players.

Discipline is the ability to stay on one's path—to choose direction over impulse, consistency over confusion, and purpose over distraction.

To a character, Discipline becomes an inner compass—something they can rely on even when emotions shift and situations change unexpectedly.

It allows them to remain focused on their path, rather than being carried away by every rising feeling or distracted by immediate rewards.

In a world where the reasons behind emotions and events are not always clear, Discipline becomes a stabilizing force, helping the character stay steady and remain true to the purpose they are guided toward.

Selflessness is the ability to care for something beyond oneself, placing a greater purpose above personal comfort or gain.

For selfless characters, the world stops revolving solely around their fears, desires, and struggles, and begins to include the needs of others. It helps the character rise above narrow impulses and choose actions that support, protect, and connect with others.

When it is no longer about "me," one begins to act without clinging to outcomes.

Together, these qualities make the character predictable in a positive way, more resilient under environmental pressure, and better able to carry out complex strategies—allowing the player to achieve goals efficiently with minimal wasted effort.

For the character, these qualities make it easier to navigate the game with clarity, resilience, and harmony, shaping a journey that feels more purposeful and stress-free—even in a world filled with uncertainty.

This clarity not only improves effectiveness in the game but also deepens a sense of inner freedom and contentment in whatever action they perform.

The Way of the Game

In a world filled with material distractions, these traits help the character make choices that lead to meaningful achievements, strong relationships, and the ability to face challenges with balance.

Over time, this naturally leads to prosperity and success, as thoughtful actions, steady focus, and care for others build trust and open new opportunities.

While happiness may not always come from external circumstances, these qualities give the character the tools to experience life in a more fulfilling, resilient, and purpose-driven way.

From the player's perspective, a character with these qualities is worth adopting, worth investing qualia in, and worth navigating the world alongside.

Players are naturally drawn to such characters because they make it easier to advance their game plans.

They adopt these characters and integrate them into their strategies—creating situations, releasing cues, and sending positive emotional signals to guide them through a game plan that not only shapes the dynamics of the game but also helps these characters become more impactful in the world around them.

Isn't this what the players want?

Isn't this what we, as characters, want?

This is how we influence our reality.

* * *

CHAPTER 13
Henry's Destiny

"We cannot escape the certainty of birth,
nor the certainty of death.

All we can shape is the life that unfolds quietly
in the space between them."

Arrival in Washida

A lot of things happened in the village over the next seven days, and the forty-day journey to Washida was not without danger, hardship, and loss.

But they eventually managed to reach the land of the Washis.

Inside Washida's thick forest, when they finally encountered the Washis and were confronted by them, a few village men lost their lives before the Washis realized that they meant no harm and had come seeking refuge in the forest.

When the Washis heard the men chant aloud the mantra the monk had given them, they took them in and led them to the Pond Village, the secret settlement of the Washis located near the northern foothills, where they met the *Mother*, the sacred leader of the tribe.

The Mother welcomed them into the village because they had chanted the forbidden mantra of Mundus Mukta.

She believed in the prophecy that one day a visitor would come who would ultimately give rise to the savior of the worlds, and that it was the duty of the Washis to protect and nurture him.

Henry and the people were given homes and food and were introduced to the incredible and awe-inspiring way of life of the Washis.

Henry's Unrest

Life began to settle for everyone, yet Henry's mind remained unsettled, and his anxiety continued to grow. His thoughts often returned to his life back on Earth.

With each passing day, his longing for home grew stronger. He wanted to return to his wife and children.

Although he and Aloha had grown closer during their journey to Washida and while settling into the Pond Village, he constantly wondered what the future truly held for them.

The closeness frightened him—not because of what it promised, but because every step toward it felt like a quiet betrayal of the life he had left behind.

He worried about the fate of the monk who had chosen to stay behind, constantly wondering what might have happened to him.

His mind could not stop questioning the prophecy of Mundus Mukta—what liberation truly meant, and whether there was genuinely a way to end the suffering of the people of Venna.

He also kept thinking about some of the visions he had seen while lost in the trance of Veda Mandala—things his mind still could not fully grasp or make sense of.

It was during this time that Henry met Theo—the crosser from Rigga.

The First Crosser

Theo was the first crosser who landed in the monk's village several years ago. When he was told that he was a crosser from another world, he was shocked and left the village in disbelief, determined to search the world for himself.

He tried to go south, but he was chased by barbaric men and nearly killed. In his struggle for survival, he eventually reached Washida, where the Washis took him in after realizing he was completely lost and exhausted with life.

The Mother, sensing a future for him among the people of Washida, allowed him to settle there and gave him a home in the woods, where he later married a Washi woman who gave birth to a boy.

When Henry and Aloha began living in the Pond Village, word slowly spread among the Washis that a crosser and a mysterious blue-eyed woman had arrived.

Many began to whisper that the ancient prophecy of Mundus Mukta might finally be nearing its fulfillment.

Theo, when he heard about Henry, came eagerly to meet him. He had always wondered whether he was living in a dream while his real physical body lay somewhere in the real world—perhaps in a coma, inside a hospital room.

He often felt as though he was waiting to be woken up one day and returned to his old life.

When he heard about another crosser, he could hardly believe it.

He had never thought that another man like him could truly exist and had long believed that he alone was destined, by sheer misfortune, to land in an imaginary world like Venna—a world that, despite everything, felt undeniably real.

For Henry, the excitement was equally overwhelming.

It took some time for both Henry and Theo to come to terms with the fact that they were indeed living in an altogether new reality, and that Venna was as real as Henry's Earth and Theo's Rigga.

An Idea Patch

During their conversation, Henry realized that Rigga was a world that had made significant advances in science and technology—far more advanced than Earth.

Theo revealed that he was a quantum system hacker and had lived the life of a con man in Rigga.

He had studied the idea of worlds being simulated as games, but he never truly believed that something like that could be achieved in reality—until he landed in Venna and met the monk.

When the monk told him that they were all living in a simulated world, Theo began to connect the dots and realized that this was exactly what quantum physicists and computer scientists in Rigga were trying hard to prove.

After his encounter with the monk, he searched for portals to travel back to Rigga, but he could not find any, as no one he met in Venna seemed to have any understanding of science or technology—even though they knew they were living in a simulated or constructed world.

Theo told Henry that, while in Rigga, he had even heard of a prototype device called a Theta Coherence Seeder, being developed by quantum computer scientists.

It was said to be capable of releasing theta waves and inducing ideas into the human brain, as part of their attempt to prove that humans were simulated beings inside a game.

"People here seem to know they live in a simulated world," Theo said, "but they can't do anything about it, right?"

Henry didn't answer, quietly piecing it all together. Rigga had taken the path of science and systems to explain existence, while Venna—having learned the truth too early—had stopped trying to control it and started trying to survive it. And that had broken them.

After a pause, he added, "Once you are born, you can only wait for your death. What else can you do?"

"The monk told me that Venna was the only world where humans live with true free will, because no players are playing the people here," Theo said.

"You know what I think? I think this Seranagu guy is just generating game points through Venna and selling them in the black market."

"Look at Venna—people killing people, war after war. For how long? Hundreds and hundreds of years?" he continued.

"Rigga used to have these wars too, but we came out of them hundreds of years ago. No one believes in wars anymore there."

"Then why are wars never-ending in this world? You see my point?" Theo said. "It looks like this world is stuck in a state of perpetual war for like forever."

"Perfect timing to get stuck, right?" Henry continued.

"Especially for this guy—if he's generating huge game points and selling them in some kind of black market."

Henry's Destiny

As Theo poured out his memories of Rigga and his theories about Seranagu and the worlds he had created, it all slowly began to make sense to Henry.

His visions from Veda Mandala also seemed to become clearer as Theo continued speaking.

He remembered the monk saying, "That was about me. This is about you," and it finally began to make sense.

He also seemed to understand what the monk had meant when he said, "Many years ago, I saw my purpose when I sat here for fourteen days."

Henry now seemed to gain a little bit of sense of his own destiny and the purpose of his arrival in Venna.

Historically, worlds have often taken entirely new directions when a new idea became widely accepted. Ideas such as art, science, freedom, and the industrial revolution, when they came, arose from different directions across the world, shifting civilizations toward entirely new paths.

What if such ideas could be spread to the characters inside the game through an update or a patch?

As his visions grew clearer, Henry began to realize that during his meditative trance in Veda Mandala, he had seen himself journeying to a new, technologically advanced world and entering a high-security facility.

He saw himself stealing a small device that looked much like the *Seeder* Theo had just talked about, trying to bring it to Veda Mandala and insert it at the center of the hexagonal plate.

It would release a Cognitive Update that would affect hundreds of millions of people across Venna, sparking the idea of freedom across its world.

He now realized that Veda Mandala was not just a Seeder amplifier but also a portal itself to travel across worlds to Rigga.

In his visions, as things became clearer while he began to connect them, Henry also saw a man helping him get inside the high-security facility by hacking into its security systems.

He saw policemen chasing them.

He saw himself driving a high-speed car, escaping the relentless chase, while the other man kept shouting about a turn they had missed as they raced against time toward a portal that was about to close.

Slowly, he began to recognize that man from his visions as Theo.

* * *

CHAPTER 14
The Life of a Character

"It is unfair to judge your past self with your present knowledge, because what you know now did not exist for you then.

Wisdom, like dawn, always comes after the night."

The Child Character

A set of unique genes, a tiny body, and a few raw, basic emotions—just enough to survive: comfort, distress, and curiosity—that's all each of us came with when we were born, with our identification code printed on our fingertips and retinas.

By the time we are five, we have many new emotions—pride, shame, guilt, empathy, love, even embarrassment.

We begin to understand how others see us, and whether what we did was good or bad.

We also start to see that the people around us have feelings just like ours. And much to our surprise, we realize we could imagine things—we could create people, places, and stories in our minds.

We also begin to realize that dreams weren't real—they were simply creations of our own imagination, flickering worlds our minds made while we slept.

By twelve, we felt we understood love better, and we felt as if we were grown up enough already.

We had more feelings now—competence, jealousy, justice and injustice, belonging and rejection.

Our schools shaped our emotions heavily. Interacting with new friends and all kinds of people, we started wanting to fit in, comparing ourselves with others, and learning what contentment, disappointment, cooperation, and failure truly felt like.

The Adolescence

By eighteen, we understood romance and intimacy. We became more self-conscious, feeling belongingness and isolation, excitement and passion in a much deeper way.

We also began to crave independence and autonomy. And with all these emotions also came confusion.

That's when we began to understand anxiety, heartbreak, betrayal, and loyalty.

And we realized that as life moved forward, we had been making choice after choice—each one shaped by the emotional impulses generated in the situations we encountered every day.

Perhaps emotions are a complex navigation system, designed to guide us through this multi-dimensional experience called life. It's like we want to reach somewhere in life in the next ten years, and emotions are what we use to steer toward that goal—making choices every single day in the hope that, eventually, all those choices will converge at that destination.

Of course, that assumes we stay fully focused all through this time, which rarely happens.

The Only Possible Way

Have you ever wondered how lifeless our lives would be without emotions?

How clueless we would become—living only for the sake of living, driven merely by our drives of survival, growth, and reproduction.

We would move through the world like robots wrapped in human flesh, functioning but never truly feeling.

We wouldn't smile, we wouldn't cry, we wouldn't feel anger or love. We would simply do what we were made to do: live until we eventually die.

Life would be much simpler, of course, like that of a fish or a bird.

We wouldn't have to make countless complex decisions every day. But then again, we wouldn't have grown the way we did either.

Perhaps that is the one reason why our creators thought of a way to create us not from a book of rules, but by allowing matter to interact only through a minimal set of fundamental rules—until we emerged as a complex system capable of navigating life using our own internal navigation system.

This is perhaps the only possible way something as complex as life could be created.

Life as a Reflection

First, the Universe was made to evolve in the same way, and then we, as life forms, were guided to evolve in the blueprint of the Universe.

In a way, our life and the Universe are the same and perhaps, our Universe is as alive as we are.

If our mind follows the blueprint of the Universe, then our emotions, too, must be formed from a few basic ones—and those basic emotions must themselves emerge from the three fundamental intrinsic impulses of life: the will to survive, to grow, and to reproduce.

And this is indeed what many lines of thought suggest.

The Alchemy of Feelings

All complex emotions appear to be derived from a few basic ones—such as joy, fear, anger, and sadness—which, in turn, trace their roots back to those three fundamental impulses.

Many complex emotions—such as love, jealousy, curiosity, trust, guilt, envy, and hope—are often understood as emerging from combinations and variations of these fundamental emotional states, blended at different intensities and shaped by thought, memory, and experience.

For instance, love can arise when joy blends with vulnerability—the fear of losing someone and the sadness of imagining life without them—creating a deep attachment that draws us toward connection.

Greed can arise when joy combines with fear: joy in gaining something, and fear of not having enough, driving us to want more than we need.

Curiosity can arise when a spark of joy meets a mild tension of uncertainty—the excitement of discovery mixed with the unknown—pushing us to explore, learn, and understand.

We all react differently to the emotions that arise within us, and those reactions shape our reality.

That is why two people can have completely different levels of acceptance—or display very different degrees of dissatisfaction—when faced with the same situation.

Each person generates a unique mix of complex emotions in response, and it is this inner emotional pattern that determines how they experience and interpret the world around them.

Gradually, as we age and gather experiences, each one of us begins to develop an emotional response pattern of our own.

This emotional setting starts to define who we are as a person. That's when we say, "Ah, Gary is a very charming fella," or "that George is a moody guy."

Your general emotional response system becomes your identity in a broader sense—shaping how others see you, how you move through the world, and what path you carve for yourself in society.

The Hidden Driver

It's amazing how a tiny extra dose of desire for fame can shift our day-to-day choices from being about growth to being about validation, and how a tiny extra dose of fear can silence the courage that once moved us forward.

A tiny dose of love can tilt our entire decision-making sequence, and a tiny dose of hatred can break bonds that took an entire lifetime to build.

And even when our conscience tells us that something we did was wrong, an extra dose of ego can easily stop us from admitting what we felt within.

It's fascinating how we, with such sound minds and formidable intellects, can be driven right and left by simple twists of emotion.

And the most unsettling part is that we don't get to choose these emotions. They come and go, reminding us that control was always more illusion than fact.

Anyone—or anything—that can inject them into us can drive us like horses pulling a chariot.

The Weaver's Plan

In the game called Universe, each one of us has a player called our Weaver, and we can be identified by our unique set of genes and bio-identification codes printed on our fingers and retinas. Emotions can be injected into us to drive us to do small, seemingly insignificant things that ultimately lead to achieving a goal for the one weaving us.

That is why emotions come and go, sometimes leaving us puzzled about why or how they arise.

We may suddenly get angry without any clear reason—or more than we should—and find ourselves saying, "I don't know why I got so angry!"

Sometimes we simply fall in love, and other times, we begin to hate something or someone over the most trivial reasons.

All of these gradually shape our reality and guide us toward our destiny—and this destiny is not fixed; it depends entirely on how we walk the path and what scheme our Weaver is attempting to unfold.

Each Weaver plays this game toward a larger goal, a goal that from our vantage point is seldom possible to anticipate.

So, all we can do is move through life, making choices guided by our emotions, following the threads we can see while trusting that unseen patterns are being woven around us.

Every milestone we reach, guided by our emotions as a character—whether success or failure—becomes a pattern revealing itself in time.

All we can do is witness these patterns unfolding without being carried away. Because there is nothing to rejoice in, and there is no reward for us as characters at the end of this road.

The Character's Destiny

As characters in the game called Universe, we are here simply to play our roles and experience life for the time we live inside the game.

Our journey is not about arriving somewhere, but about how we move through the threads, the depth of emotions we touch, and the impressions we leave behind.

Every choice, every emotion, every moment of awareness is the true essence of playing this game of life.

At the end, all characters die.

* * *

CHAPTER 15
Henry's Death

"We move forward not because we know everything,
but because we believe we know enough.

In hindsight, the things we doubted most
often make the most sense."

Henry's Plan

To Henry, it all began to grow clear. He started to feel strongly within his mind that his purpose was to liberate the people of Venna from the oppression and suffering they were enduring.

In his mind, he began to build a plan—a plan to travel across worlds to Rigga with Theo through the portal of Veda Mandala.

He would retrieve the Seeder, and release the missing Cognition Patch into the world of Venna.

This, Henry believed, would gradually set off a series of events and revolutions, ultimately uprooting the idea of dictatorship from both its people and their world.

"It is what liberation means," Henry quietly said to himself.

"If I could bring about liberation, there would be no need for the Mundus Mukta, and I could finally go back home. That's what the vision is all about."

He turned to Theo and, in a tone of confidence and excitement, said, "I know what we should do."

The Truth Henry Didn't See

It is in our nature to think that we know everything, even when we are unaware of how little we truly know. And this is not always a bad thing.

Often, it gives us the courage to move forward where we might have otherwise stopped or paused with doubt and disbelief.

Henry was confident that he could liberate the people of Venna from their suffering. To him, that vision seemed perfectly clear and firmly set in stone.

Henry was willing to face the danger and take the chance because he now truly believes that when all that is over, he will be able to go back home and be together with his wife and children once again.

But little did Henry know what his visions would slowly reveal to him as he traveled through the portal of Veda Mandala.

Gradually but surely, he would come to realize the truth—that the only way he could fully return to his family on Earth was through his death in the reality of Venna.

Henry will have to endure a real death in one reality for his consciousness to get back to the other.

Because his visions in Veda Mandala were blurred by his rising and falling emotions, Henry failed to grasp what they had truly revealed about the moment he crossed into Venna.

What he did not yet realize was that during the storm—when panic took over—his consciousness had split into two.

And while one continued along its usual reality on Earth, the other took the path of the crosser and landed in Venna's reality near the lakeside village.

Gradually, Henry will have to realize that the "Henry" he saw in his visions—playing with his children alongside his beloved wife back home—was not his future, but another version of him: undoubtedly real, unaware, and separate from the reality he is now in.

And when that realization comes, Henry will have to decide whether he is truly willing to give up his present reality to discover if another reality awaits him on the other side, and whether his present consciousness would merge with the one already present in Earth's reality.

Would Henry be willing to give up one life that he certainly knew was real, for another that he was not so sure of?

Would it be a chance Henry was willing to take?

And if Henry succeeded in bringing about a revolution against the Dictators and the people were liberated from their oppressive rulers, would that translate to true liberation for the people of Venna?

And if it indeed did, what would become of the prophecy of Mundus Mukta?

* * *

To those whose quest never dies.

To those who refuse to believe everything they are told.

9 789356 551473

Printed at Repro India Ltd.